WITHDRAWN

Wonderful You

Written by Lisa Graff · Illustrated by Ramona Kaulitzki

PHILOMEL BOOKS

Before you were with us, we already knew
that the thing most worth doing was waiting for you.

When you were a sweet pea (so tiny—it's true!),
we cheered and we chattered and waited for you.

When you were a fig, we had dreams—quite a few!
We wondered and wagered and waited for you.

When you were a plum, and we hadn't a clue,
we read and we researched and waited for you.

When you were a lemon,
we followed your cue.
We watched and we whispered
and waited for you.

When you were a mango, we worked while you grew—
we fixed and we folded and waited for you.

When you were a grapefruit,
who flipped at our coo,
we whistled and waltzed and
we waited for you.

When you were an eggplant,
we called in our crew.
We painted and prepped and
we waited for you.

When you were a cabbage (and tireless, too!),
we woke up with, warbled at, waited for you.

When you were a pineapple, time nearly flew.
We danced and we dreamt and we waited for you.

When you were a pumpkin,
we had so much to do!
We washed and we worked
and we waited for you.

Then, wrinkled and wriggly, you made your debut,
and our whole world changed when we set eyes on you.

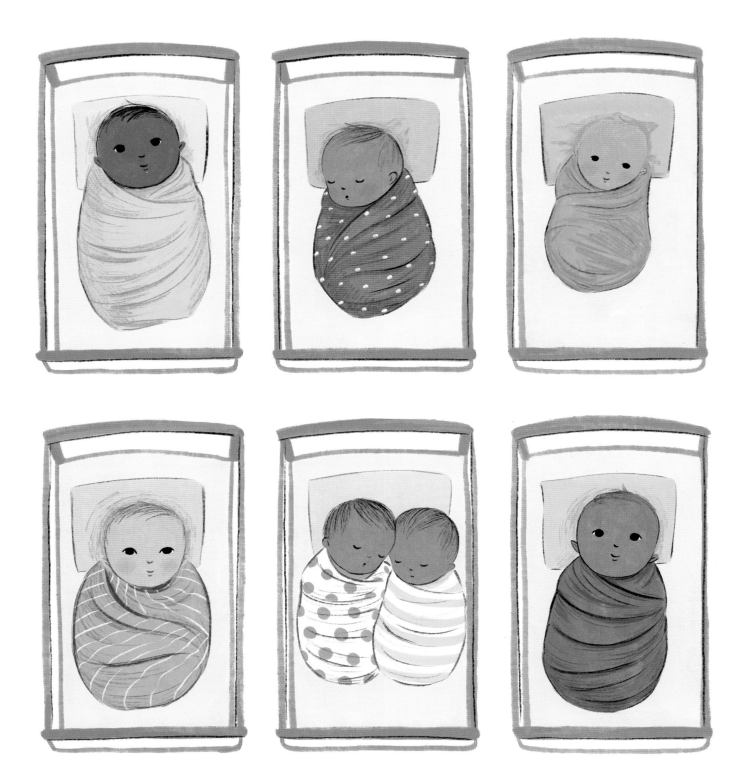

Not berry nor apple nor sweet honeydew,

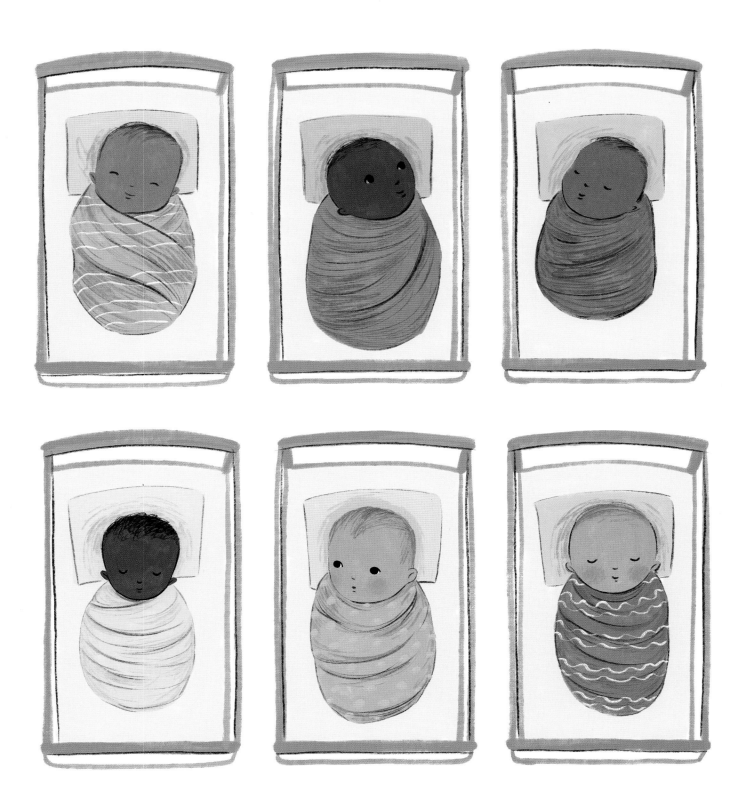

just wee little, wry little, wonderful you.

And now that you're here, and our waiting is through,
you're more than we wished for—you're utterly you.

Any way that you grow, any path you pursue, you've been loved.

You are loved.

We'll always love you.

For L & N—L.G.
For my parents—R.K.

PHILOMEL BOOKS
An imprint of Penguin Random House LLC, New York

Text copyright © 2020 by Lisa Graff. Illustrations copyright © 2020 by Ramona Kaulitzki.

Philomel Books is a registered trademark of Penguin Random House LLC.

Visit us online at penguinrandomhouse.com

Library of Congress Cataloging-in-Publication Data is available.

ISBN 9781984837387

Manufactured in China.

10 9 8 7 6 5 4 3 2 1

Edited by Jill Santopolo.
Design by Ellice M. Lee.
Text set in Mrs. Eaves OT.
The art was done in digitally in Photoshop.